Read to Me, Grandma

Read to Me, Grandma

EDITED BY GLORYA HALE

JellyBean Press
New York • Avenel, New Jersey

For Caroline Trovato

Copyright © 1993 by
Random House Value Publishing, Inc.
All rights reserved

First published in 1993 by JellyBean Press,
distributed by Random House Value Publishing, Inc.
40 Engelhard Avenue
Avenel, New Jersey 07001

Designed by Liz Trovato

Manufactured in the United States

Library of Congress Cataloging-in-Publication Data

Read to Me Grandma / edited by Glorya Hale; illustrated
by Jesse Willcox Smith and Charles Robinson.
p. cm.
Summary : an illustrated collection of fairy tales, fables,
and poems by such authors as Robert Louis Stevenson and
James Whitcomb Riley.
1. Children's literature. [1. Literature—Collections.]
I. Hale, Glorya II. Smith, Jesse Willcox, ill.
III. Robinson, Charles, 1931- ill.
PZ5.R19843 1993
808.8'99282—dc20
93-3384
CIP
AC

ISBN: 0-517-09348-0

8 7 6 5 4 3 2

CONTENTS

INTRODUCTION

This is a book for you to share with your grandchildren on a rainy afternoon, at bedtime, perhaps at the beach or at a picnic, whenever a child says, "Please read to me, Grandma." It is a delightful collection of stories, fables, and poems from your own childhood that you can now enjoy again with the youngest generation.

Surely you remember how pleased and amazed you were when Cinderella's fairy godmother transformed the poor little scullery maid and sent her off to the ball. Undoubtedly, you can recall your fear that Jack wouldn't reach the beanstalk before the wicked giant caught him. And certainly you've not forgotten the beautiful princess, Briar Rose, who slept for a hundred years, or Rose-Red and Rose-White, the sisters who befriended a talking bear. Here, too, you'll find the story of "Beauty and the Beast" as it was written by Charles Perrault.

Also included are a number of Aesop's best fables and a selection of charming poems, including five from A *Child's Garden of Verses* by Robert Louis Stevenson and James Whitcomb Riley's hilarious "The Bear Story."

This beautifully designed book, with its charming illustrations by such well-known artists as Jessie Willcox Smith, Anne Anderson, and Margaret W. Tarrant, will surely reawaken memories of your own childhood, of the pleasures of learning to read and of being read to. And together you and the children who are very special to you can visit enchanted lands—of good fairies, and some who are wicked, of handsome princes and beautiful princesses, of dwarfs and giants, of magic spells and wondrous imaginings—and share moments that will become their golden memories.

GLORYA HALE

Jack and the Beanstalk

ACK was the only son of a poor widow. He was a lazy boy and, as time went on, he grew lazier and lazier, and his mother grew poorer and poorer, until she had nothing left in the world but a cow.

One day Jack's mother said to him, "Tomorrow you must take the cow to market, and the more money you get for her the better."

The next morning Jack got up earlier than usual, hung his cowhorn around his neck, and started for market with the cow. On the way he met a butcher.

"Good morning, my lad," said the butcher. "And where may you be going?"

"To market," replied Jack.

"And what may you be going to market for?" asked the butcher.

"To sell the cow," said Jack.

"Just look at what I have here," said the butcher and held out his hand. In it lay some strange-looking beans. "If you give me the cow, I'll give you the beans."

That would be a good bargain, thought Jack. So he exchanged the cow for the beans and returned home to his mother.

"Look," he said gleefully, as he poured the beans into her lap. "I have got all these in exchange for the cow."

"You bad, stupid boy!" exclaimed the angry mother. "Now we shall have to starve." And she took the beans and flung them out the open window.

There was no food for supper that night and the next morning Jack woke early, feeling very hungry. But what was that dark shadow across his window? Jack went over to see. It seemed as if a tall tree grew where no tree had been before.

Jack ran to the garden and found that the shadow was cast not by a tree, but by a beanstalk. This beanstalk had sprung up during the night from the beans his mother had thrown out the window. The enormous stalks had entwined to form a kind of ladder, the top of which seemed to be lost in the clouds.

Jack began to climb the beanstalk. He climbed and he climbed and he climbed. And all the time he grew hungrier and hungrier and hungrier. Finally, at midday, he reached the top of the beanstalk and stepped off into a wild, bare country. Jack walked on until he met an old woman. He thought he had never seen anyone who looked quite so old.

"Good morning, Jack," she said.

How in the world does she know my name? thought Jack to himself, but he only said, "Good morning, Dame."

"I know who you are, and where you come from, and how you got here, and all about you," said the old woman. "And I will tell you where you are and what you are to do."

Then she told Jack that he was in a country that belonged to a wicked giant. This giant had killed Jack's father and stolen all he possessed. Jack had only been a baby at that time, and his mother had been too distressed to speak to him about it since. But that was why she was so poor. The old woman told Jack that he must punish this giant if his mother and he were ever to be happy again. The task was a difficult one, but Jack must be brave and succeed. Then the old woman went on her way and he went on his.

Toward evening Jack came to the door of a castle. He blew his horn. A woman opened the door.

"I am very tired and hungry," said Jack. "Can you give me supper and a night's lodging?"

"You little know, my poor lad, what you ask," said the woman. "My husband is a giant. He eats people. He would be sure to find you and eat you for supper. No, no, it would never do." And she shut the door.

But Jack felt too tired to go another step, so he blew his horn again and when the woman again opened the door he begged to be fed and given a place to rest.

The giant's wife began to cry, but at last Jack persuaded her to let him come in. She led him past dungeons where many men and women were imprisoned. Then they reached the kitchen. Soon Jack was enjoying a good

meal so much that he forgot to be afraid. But before he had finished, there was a loud knock and in a moment the giant's wife had popped him into the oven to hide.

The giant walked in and sniffed the air. "I smell a human being," he said.

"You are dreaming," said his wife and the giant sniffed no more, but sat down to supper.

Through a hole in the oven door Jack peeped at the giant. He was surprised to see how enormous he was and how much and how quickly he ate. When he had finished eating, he said to his wife, "Bring me my hen." His wife brought a beautiful hen and put it on the table.

"Lay!" shouted the giant, and the hen laid an egg of solid gold.

"Another!" roared the giant, and another golden egg was laid. And again and again the giant gave the order in a voice of thunder and the hen obeyed, until twelve golden eggs were laid on the table. Then the giant went to sleep and snored so loudly that the whole castle shook.

Jack did not let this chance to escape pass. He crept out of the oven, seized the hen, and ran off as fast as he could. On and on he ran, until he reached the top of the beanstalk. Then he climbed quickly down and carried the wonderful hen to his mother.

Day after day the hen laid its golden eggs, and by selling them Jack and his mother became very rich.

For some months Jack and his mother lived happily together. But Jack longed for more adventure, and so early one morning he again climbed the beanstalk. When he reached the top he stepped off, followed the same path as before, and arrived at the giant's castle. This time he had disguised himself, so when the giant's wife came to the door she did not recognize the boy she had hidden in the oven.

"I should be glad of food and rest, good woman, for I am hungry and tired," said Jack.

"You can't get that here," answered the giant's wife. "I once took in a tired and hungry lad and he stole my husband's precious hen that lays golden eggs."

Then Jack pretended to think the boy who stole the hen must be a very bad boy. And he spoke so pleasantly to the giant's wife that she began to feel it would be unkind not to give him a meal. So she let him come in. After Jack had had a good supper the giant's wife hid him in a cupboard. None too soon either, for in stalked the giant sniffing the air.

"I smell a human being," he said.

"Perfect nonsense," said his wife as she placed the giant's supper on the table.

After supper the giant roared, "Fetch me my money bags!" His wife brought them and Jack, peeping out of the cupboard, thought, I am sure those money bags belonged to my father. And he was quite right.

The giant emptied the gold and silver coins out of the bags, counted them over and over again, and then put them back. Very soon he was fast asleep.

As soon as Jack heard the giant's loud snores he stole out of the cupboard, and, with the bags slung over his shoulder, ran off as fast as he could. On and on he ran, until he reached the top of the beanstalk. Then he climbed quickly down and took the money bags to his mother.

Jack and his mother were now extremely well off, but Jack felt that the giant had not yet been punished enough. But it was some time before he dared venture again into the giant's country.

At last, however, Jack made up his mind to disguise himself quite differently, and see if he could again persuade the giant's wife to let him enter the castle. He climbed the beanstalk, followed the same path, and arrived at the castle door. The giant's wife did not recognize Jack. He begged for some food and a place to rest for the night.

"No, no," she said, "you can't come in here. The last tired lads that I took in were thieves. One stole a golden hen, and the other two money bags. No, no, you can't come in."

But Jack begged and begged, and at last the giant's wife took pity on him and, after giving him supper, hid him in an empty barrel. Soon the giant came home and, sniffing the air, roared, "I smell a human being!"

"A human being?" said his wife. "Impossible!" and she put his supper on the table.

After supper the giant shouted, "Fetch me my harp!" The giant's wife brought a beautiful harp and put it on the table.

"Play," said the giant, and the harp began to play of its own accord. And it played and played until it had played the giant to sleep. Then Jack, hearing the thundering snores of the giant, jumped out of the barrel and seized the harp. But he had no sooner touched it than it called out, "Master, master!" for it was a magic harp.

Jack, terrified, ran for his life in the direction of the beanstalk. Looking behind he saw the giant striding after him. Jack then ran as he had never run before and safely reached the top of the beanstalk. He climbed down as quick as lightning, and then called out, "Mother, mother, the axe. Quick—the giant's coming!"

Then Jack's mother ran more quickly than she had run since she was a girl, and gave the axe to Jack. With one blow he cut down the beanstalk. It happened as he hoped, for there was a tremendous thud, and the giant fell headlong from the top and now lay dead in the garden.

Jack and his mother lived together for many, many years. He continued to be a good and diligent son and they were always very happy.

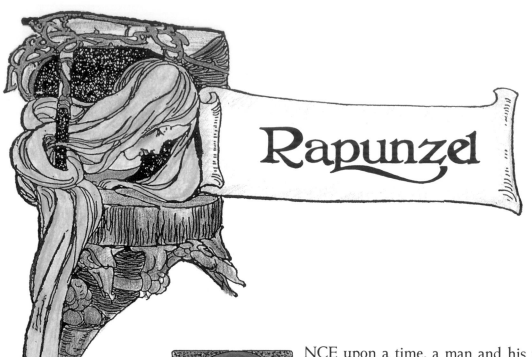

Rapunzel

NCE upon a time, a man and his wife lived happily together. They had all that they could wish for, except a little child, and they often said, "Oh, if only we had a little daughter!" They never gave up hope that some day the little daughter would come.

A window, at the back of their house, looked into a splendid garden, which was surrounded by high walls. Nobody would have dared to climb these walls, because the garden belonged to a powerful and wicked witch who was feared by everyone.

One day the woman was standing at the window that overlooked the garden. She saw some tempting salad greens, of the kind called rapunzel, growing there. They looked so fresh and green that she longed to taste them. Each time she looked at the greens she wanted them more and more. Soon they became the only thing that she did want to eat, and because she could not get them she became pale and thin. Her husband could not understand why she was so changed, but one day she told him. "I shall die," she said, "unless I taste those salad greens."

"Rather than let you die, I shall climb the witch's wall, let it cost what it may," said her husband. So at twilight he climbed over the wall, picked a handful of the greens, and took them to his wife. She made a salad with them and ate it at once. She enjoyed the salad so much that the next day her longing was even greater and she begged her husband to go again into the garden. When he saw that she would make herself ill unless he went, at twilight he again climbed the wall. But to his horror he found himself face to face with the witch.

"How dare you come into my garden? How dare you steal my greens?" she demanded.

"They are for my wife," answered the man. "I was afraid she would die if she could not have them."

"I see," said the witch. "Well, your wife must not die. Take as much of the greens as you like. But promise this: If you have a little daughter, you must give her to me. I will be a mother to her." The poor husband promised, for he was much too afraid of the witch, and too anxious to take the greens, to think of what his words might mean.

After some time the woman had a daughter. The witch quickly appeared and carried off the baby girl, to whom she gave the name Rapunzel.

Rapunzel grew to be a most beautiful girl. When she was fifteen years old, the witch shut her up in a tower that stood in the middle of a great forest. How she did this we do not know, for the tower had neither staircase nor doors and only one little window way up near the top. When the witch wanted to enter the tower, she stood at the foot of it and called:

> "Rapunzel, Rapunzel, let down your hair,
> That I may climb without a stair."

The girl had wonderful hair. It was so long and as fine as spun gold. When she heard the witch's voice, she threw her long braid over the little balcony at her window, so that it reached the ground beneath. Then she held the top of the braid tight with both hands, and the witch climbed up.

After several years had passed, a king's son, riding through the forest, heard in the distance a song so lovely that he stood still to listen. Where could it come from? He rode in the direction of the sound and came to the tower. He tried to enter it, but neither door nor staircase could he find. He looked up at the pretty window. No one was to be seen. Yet there was no doubt that the singer of the song was in the tower.

The prince rode home, but he felt as if he should like to listen to that song forever. The next day he went again to the forest, and the next, and the next, always hoping to hear that girl's voice singing her sweet song and wondering if one day she might come to the window. Sometimes he heard not a sound, but often her song floated down to him. Each time he heard it the voice seemed sweeter than the last, and he longed more and more to see the girl who sang.

One day, as he sat behind a tree, he saw the witch come to the tower and he heard her call:

> "Rapunzel, Rapunzel, let down your hair,
> That I may climb without a stair."

Then the prince saw the long golden braid thrown over the little balcony at the window. It reached to the ground beneath. Looking up he saw a beautiful girl. She held the top of her braid tight with both hands, and the witch climbed up on it.

"If that is the ladder by which one may enter the tower, I mean to climb it," said the prince to himself, as he rode home.

The next evening, at twilight, he stood at the foot of the tower and called:

> "Rapunzel, Rapunzel, let down your hair,
> That.I may climb without a stair."

In a moment the braid was thrown down and up the prince climbed.

When Rapunzel saw him she was very frightened, for she had never seen a man before. But he talked so kindly to her that she soon lost her fear. He told her how her song had led him to the tower and made him long to see her. Then he told her how, after many a month's waiting, he had seen her, and how that had made him long to speak to her. And now that he had spoken to her he loved her dearly and wanted to marry her.

Rapunzel was startled because it had all happened so suddenly. She looked at the handsome young prince, in his blue suit, with its striped sash and lace ruffle. He, too, was golden-haired and on his head he wore a black hat with

a large black plume. His voice was so kind and his way was so gentle that Rapunzel felt sure she would be happy with him.

"Yes, I will marry you, Prince," she said. "But how am I to escape from this tower?" The two thought and thought, and at last Rapunzel had an idea.

"Come to see me each evening, Prince, for the witch comes only in the day. And bring me, every time you come, a skein of silk. I will weave it into a ladder. When it is long enough, I will climb down and you can carry me off on your horse." Then the prince kissed Rapunzel, let himself down by her hair, and waved good-bye.

The witch knew nothing of their meetings, until one day Rapunzel said, "How is it, good mother, that you are so much harder to pull up than the prince?"

"What!" said the witch. "You naughty, wicked girl! I thought I had kept you from all the world. You have deceived me." And in her anger the witch seized a pair of scissors and cut off Rapunzel's braid, which fell to the ground. The witch then took the long braid and fastened it securely to the window-sill, so that she and Rapunzel could descend in safety. She then took the poor girl into a wilderness and left her there, lonely and miserable.

The witch returned to the tower in the evening. She climbed up the ladder of hair and pulled it in after her. Soon the prince called:

"Rapunzel, Rapunzel, let down your hair,

That I may climb without a stair."

And the witch let down the hair.

The prince mounted and found himself face to face not with his dearest Rapunzel, but with the witch, who was staring at him with angry eyes.

"Ah," she cried mockingly, "you have come to fetch your lady, but the beautiful bird has flown the nest and will sing no more. The cat got her and soon it will scratch out your eyes. You will never see Rapunzel again."

In despair, the prince sprang from the high window. The fall did not kill him, but his eyes were scratched by the thorns among which he fell. Blind, he wandered through the forest with nothing to eat but roots and berries. His one thought was of Rapunzel.

One day the prince reached the wilderness where Rapunzel was living. He heard a voice singing the same song that he had so often listened to beneath the tower. He followed in its direction and, as he approached, Rapunzel recognized him. She put her arms around him and wept. Two big teardrops fell upon the prince's eyes and they immediately grew quite clear, and he saw as well as ever.

Then, hand in hand, they went together to the prince's kingdom, where they were married amid great joy and lived happily ever after.

The Grasshopper and the Ants

One fine day in winter some ants were busy drying their store of corn, which had got rather damp during a long spell of rain. Presently up came a grasshopper and begged them to spare her a few grains, "For," she said, "I'm simply starving."

The ants stopped work for a moment, though this was against their principles. "May we ask," said they, "what you were doing with yourself all last summer? Why didn't you collect a store of food for the winter?"

"The fact is," replied the grasshopper, "I was so busy singing that I hadn't the time."

"If you spent the summer singing," replied the ants, "you can't do better than spend the winter dancing." And they chuckled and went on with their work.

AESOP

The Dog in the Manger

A dog was lying in a manger on the hay which had been put there for the cattle, and when they came and tried to eat he growled and snapped at them and wouldn't let them get at their food. "What a selfish beast," said one of the cows to her companions. "He can't eat himself and yet he won't let those eat who can."

AESOP

Cinderella

E do not know what Cinderella was called when she was a little girl and her own mother was alive. It was after her mother was dead, and she was a young woman, that we hear of her first. It was then that she was called Cinderella. Her father had married again and his new wife had two daughters who were very unkind to his child. When she was not hard at work the poor girl would sit alone in the chimney corner among the cinders. And that is how she got the name Cinderella.

The stepsisters made Cinderella work from morning until night, while they amused themselves. She carried the coal and she washed the dishes. She scrubbed, and she swept, and she dusted, and she mended. She waited, too, on her cross stepsisters. When night came, poor Cinderella went to a cold, lonely attic, to sleep on a straw mattress. But her sisters had a warm, comfortable bedroom.

Now, the king of the country in which they lived was going to give two balls, because his son, the prince, was coming of age. The stepsisters were invited, and they were so excited that they could talk of nothing but the balls from morning until night. Of course, Cinderella had no invitation, for she was never seen, except at work, or waiting on her stepsisters, and so she was often taken for their maid.

When the night of the first ball came, Cinderella helped her sisters to put on their finery, and she fixed their hair, and she fastened their gloves. How she would have liked to go too! What joy, she thought, to wear a pretty dress, and drive in a carriage, and see the inside of a palace, and perhaps be spoken to by the prince! And as Cinderella thought of these things tears ran down her cheeks.

"What are you crying for?" asked the younger sister crossly.

"Oh, I want to—I mean, it must be so wonderful to go to a ball," said Cinderella.

"You go to a ball! Nobody would look at you," the elder sister answered. Then they drove off in their grand carriage and poor Cinderella sat down among the cinders. She hid her face in her hands and cried as if her heart would break.

"What is the matter, my dear?" asked a kind voice.

Cinderella jumped up quickly and made a curtsy to the little old lady who had spoken so gently. She explained that she was Cinderella's fairy godmother and, like all fairies, could appear or disappear at any moment.

"Oh, godmother, I want—" But Cinderella could say no more

"You want to go to the ball," said the fairy godmother. "Very well, my dear, you shall go. Only do exactly as I tell you. First, run and find me a big pumpkin."

Cinderella brought a large pumpkin from the garden. The fairy godmother touched it with her wand and it was at once changed into a gilded carriage.

"Now run and fetch me the mousetrap from the pantry."

Cinderella brought the mousetrap. There were six mice in it. With one touch of the fairy wand the door of the trap opened. Out ran the six mice one after another. And one after another they were touched with the magic wand and changed into beautiful gray horses.

"Next run and fetch me the rat trap."

Cinderella brought the rat trap. There was a rat in it. Again a touch of the fairy wand opened the door and as the rat ran out it was changed into a tall coachman in gay livery.

"One more errand, my dear," said the fairy godmother. "Bring me the two lizards that are behind the cucumber frame."

Cinderella brought the lizards. The fairy godmother again lifted her wand and with a single touch the lizards were changed into two grand footmen.

But after her godmother had worked all these wonders, Cinderella still looked sad. And the fairy understood why.

"One more touch of my magic wand," she said, and in a moment Cinderella looked like a lovely princess. She wore the daintiest pink and white dress, red roses crowned her golden hair, and slippers of sparkling glass were on her little feet.

"Good-bye, my dear," said the fairy godmother. "But remember this— you must leave the palace before the clock strikes twelve, or the coach will become a pumpkin again, the horses mice, the coachman a rat, the footmen lizards, and you yourself the ragged girl you were."

Then she kissed Cinderella and waved her wand as the carriage rolled off.

So Cinderella drove in state to the ball and the prince himself came to help her out of the carriage and led her to the ballroom. He thought he had never seen so beautiful a princess, and he and the wicked sisters and everyone who was at the ball wondered who this lovely young woman could be. The prince danced with her oftener than with anyone else. At a quarter to twelve Cinderella remembered her godmother's warning and left the palace. Just as the clock struck twelve she reached home. The fairy awaited her. In a moment she was changed into the ragged girl and sat down in the chimney corner.

When Cinderella's sisters came home they found her among the cinders, rubbing her eyes, and pretending she had been asleep. She heard them talk of the beautiful princess and wonder who she was.

The next night the king gave the second ball and Cinderella again helped her sisters to get ready. Then again she sat down among the cinders. Soon her godmother appeared and the fairy wand worked the same wonders as before.

And Cinderella, looking even more beautiful than on the first night, rolled off in her gilded carriage.

The prince danced with her the whole evening, and she was so happy that she did not notice how time was flying. Suddenly she glanced at the clock. One minute to twelve! Without saying good-bye to the prince, Cinderella

ran from the palace as quickly as she could. But she had gone no farther than the hall door when the last stroke of twelve sounded. Immediately she was changed into a ragged girl. Nothing was left of her grandeur except the glass slippers and, in her hurry, Cinderella dropped one of them. She did not dare to turn to look for it, but ran on and on until she reached home.

The prince did not know why the beautiful young woman had left him so suddenly. He ran after her and, although he did not find her, he found the little glass slipper she had dropped. He picked it up and put it in his pocket.

The next day a herald went through the city and cried out that the prince wanted to find the young woman who owned the glass slipper, since he wanted to marry her. All the ladies who had been at the ball were asked to try on the slipper. Each lady tried to squeeze her foot into the dainty little glass slipper, but not one of them could.

When the herald came to the home of Cinderella's father, the cross sisters each had their turn, but they did not succeed to get the slipper on. Just as the herald was leaving, Cinderella came in with her mending.

"Oh, let me try," she said.

"You!" said the elder sister. "You!" said the younger. And they each pointed at her ragged dress and laughed a loud, ugly laugh. But the herald said that Cinderella should try. The slipper fit her exactly. Then Cinderella drew the other glass slipper from her pocket. To her sisters that seemed like magic.

But they were to get a still greater surprise. The fairy godmother suddenly appeared. She touched Cinderella with her wand and in a moment the ragged girl was changed into a beautiful princess. And as the sisters gazed in wonder, they saw that this beautiful princess was the same lovely young woman that everyone had admired at the ball. They then fell on their knees and begged Cinderella to forgive them. And she did and was kinder to them than they deserved.

Then Cinderella said good-bye to them all and went with the herald to the palace. The prince met her and soon they were married and lived happily ever after.

The Wind.

I saw you toss the kites on high
And blow the birds about the sky;
And all around I heard you pass,
Like ladies' skirts across the grass—
   O wind, a-blowing all day long,
   O wind, that sings so loud a song!

I saw the different things you did,
But always you yourself you hid.
I felt you push, I heard you call,
I could not see yourself at all—
   O wind, a-blowing all day long,
   O wind, that sings so loud a song!

O you that are so strong and cold,
O blower, are you young or old?
Are you a beast of field and tree,
Or just a stronger child than me?
   O wind, a-blowing all day long,
   O wind, that sings so loud a song!

ROBERT LOUIS STEVENSON

MY SHADOW

I have a little shadow that goes in and out with me,
And what can be the use of him is more than I can see.
He is very, very like me from the heels up to the head;
And I see him jump before me, when I jump into my bed.

The funniest thing about him is the way he likes to grow—
Not at all like proper children, which is always very slow;
For he sometimes shoots up taller like an india-rubber ball,
And sometimes gets so little that there's none of him at all.

He hasn't got a notion of how children ought to play,
And can only make a fool of me in every sort of way.
He stays so close beside me, he's a coward you can see;
I'd think shame to stick to nursie as that shadow sticks to me!

One morning very early, before the sun was up,
I rose and found the shining dew on every buttercup;
But my lazy little shadow, like an arrant sleepy-head,
Had stayed at home behind me and was fast asleep in bed.

ROBERT LOUIS STEVENSON

Snowdrop

NE winter day, long, long ago, a queen sat by the window sewing. Every now and again she lifted her eyes to gaze at the fast-falling snow. Suddenly she pricked her finger and three drops of blood fell. "Oh," sighed the queen, "how I wish I could have a little daughter, as white as snow, as red as blood, and as black as this ebony window frame."

Soon afterward the queen did have a baby girl and her skin was as white as snow, her cheeks were as rosy as the drops of blood, and her hair was as black as ebony. The queen called her little girl Snowdrop. But, sad to say, Snowdrop's mother died and a year later the king brought home another queen.

This new queen was very beautiful and she could not bear to think that anyone else was as lovely. She had a magic mirror that answered her questions, and often she asked—

"Mirror, mirror on the wall,
Am I most beautiful of all?"

And the mirror always answered—

"Thou, Queen, art fairest of beauties all."

One day, when Snowdrop was almost a young woman, and the queen asked her mirror the usual question, it replied—

"Though fair and lovely is the queen,
Snowdrop's lovelier far, I ween."

The queen was very angry indeed. And each day she grew angrier and angrier, until at last she told one of her huntsmen to take Snowdrop far into the heart of a wild wood and kill her. So the huntsman took Snowdrop to the wood and when they were where no one could hear or see them, he took out his knife to kill the girl. But Snowdrop begged him to save her, and when she promised to go farther into the wood, and never again return home, the huntsman let her run away.

All day Snowdrop journeyed on, over sharp stones and through prickly bushes, often hearing the roar of wild beasts around her. Then she climbed hill after hill. By evening she was thoroughly tired out. It was with great joy that she finally came to a little cottage and she went in to rest.

Everything in this cottage was wonderfully tidy. On a table was spread a clean white cloth. On the cloth were seven little plates and on each plate was a little loaf of bread. There were also seven little knives and forks and seven little wine glasses, each filled with wine. Then, along the wall, there were seven neat little beds, each with a snow-white counterpane.

Snowdrop was hungry as well as tired, so she ate a little piece off each loaf and drank a little out of each wine glass. Then she lay down on one of the beds. But she was not comfortable on it, so she tried another, and then another. It was not until she reached the seventh bed that she said her prayers and settled down to sleep.

When it was quite dark, the masters of the cottage came home. They were seven dwarfs who lived among the mountains, digging and searching for gold. The dwarfs lighted their seven candles and immediately saw that someone had been in the cottage since they left it.

"Who has been sitting on my stool?" said the first.

"Who has eaten off my plate?" said the second.

"Who has been picking my loaf?" said the third.

"Who has been meddling with my spoon?" said the fourth.

"Who has been fiddling with my fork?" said the fifth.

"Who has been cutting with my knife?" said the sixth.

"Who has been drinking my wine?" said the seventh.

Then the first dwarf noticed a hollow in his bed and called out, "Who has been sleeping in my bed?" "And who has been sleeping in mine," "and

mine," "and mine," "and mine," "and mine?" called out the other dwarfs.

But the seventh dwarf cried, "Look, look!" for he saw Snowdrop sound asleep in his bed.

The seven dwarfs then held up their seven candles that they might throw their light on the girl. "Oh, what a lovely child!" they all cried in a breath. Then they went about on tiptoe, saying nothing but "hush," in case they should wake her. And when bedtime came the seventh dwarf did not disturb

Snowdrop, but slept an hour with each of the other dwarfs until the night had passed.

When morning came Snowdrop woke and was startled and frightened to see the seven little men. But they spoke kindly to her, and asked her name.

"Snowdrop," she said.

"But how did you find your way here, Snowdrop?" they asked.

Snowdrop then told them of her jealous stepmother, who wanted to kill her, and of the huntsman who spared her life, and of her wanderings through the wood until she reached their cottage.

The dwarfs felt sorry for the pretty girl, and told her that if she would cook and wash and mend for them, and keep their little house tidy, she might live with them and they would take care of her. And Snowdrop agreed gladly.

The dwarfs had to be out at work all day. Before they went they warned Snowdrop to let no one come into the cottage, "because," they said, "your stepmother is sure to try to find you and harm you."

But the queen felt quite certain that Snowdrop was dead, and quite happy to think that she was now the most beautiful person alive. One day she thought she would like to hear this from her magic mirror, so she asked—

"Mirror, mirror on the wall,
Am I most beautiful of all?"

It almost took the queen's breath away to hear the mirror's answer—

"Thou art the fairest here, O Queen;
But Snowdrop over the hills, I ween,
In the little house where the seven dwarfs are,
Is good and younger and fairer far."

Then the queen made up her mind to find Snowdrop and kill her. But how was she to manage? She thought and thought and at last decided to go as a poor old woman selling wares. She knew Snowdrop had a kind heart and was sorry for the poor.

After dressing in old clothes and painting her face, the wicked queen went

through the wood and over the hills and finally arrived at the cottage. Then she called out—"Wares to sell. White laces, blue laces, bobbins, and silk! Who will buy my wares?"

Snowdrop put her head out the window, and thought to herself, It can do no harm to let this poor woman come in. So she unlocked the door and bought some blue laces from the poor woman.

"Let me lace your dress with one of them," said the woman. Snowdrop agreed, but the cruel queen pulled the laces so tight that Snowdrop could not breathe. She fell on the floor as if dead.

"Now I'm the fairest in the land," said the queen with a loud, ugly laugh, and off she went.

SNOWDROP

When the seven dwarfs came home that night, how alarmed they were to find poor Snowdrop lying seemingly lifeless on the floor! They lifted her up and when they saw how tightly the lace was drawn they cut it. Very soon Snowdrop began to breathe, and gradually she came back to life. When the dwarfs heard what had happened they said, "The old woman must have been the queen herself," and again they warned Snowdrop to let no one come into the cottage.

As soon as the wicked queen reached home, she went straight to her magic mirror, and again it said—

"Thou art the fairest here, O Queen;
But Snowdrop over the hills, I ween,
In the little house where the seven dwarfs are,
Is good and younger and fairer far."

When the queen learned that Snowdrop was still alive, she flew into a terrible rage, and said, "I'll make sure the next time." Then she dressed as a quite different old woman, and painted herself in another way, and put among her wares a poisoned comb.

Again the wicked woman went to the dwarfs' cottage and there she called out, "Wares to sell! Wares to sell!"

"I dare not let you come in," called Snowdrop from the window.

"But look at my beautiful combs," said the woman. And the combs did look so beautiful that Snowdrop opened the door and let the woman put one in her hair. It was the poisoned one, and immediately Snowdrop fell to the ground.

"I've done it this time," muttered the old woman and off she went.

Fortunately, the dwarfs came home early that evening and when they saw Snowdrop again lying as if dead on the floor, they knew the queen had been there. They quickly found the comb. As soon as they had drawn it from Snowdrop's hair she was herself again and told them what had happened. Once more the dwarfs warned her that she must on no account let anyone come into the cottage.

On reaching home the wicked queen again went straight to her mirror, and once more it said—

> "Thou art the fairest here, O Queen;
> But Snowdrop over the hills, I ween,
> In the little house where the seven dwarfs are,
> Is good and younger and fairer far."

Then the queen danced with rage. "Snowdrop shall die, even if it costs me my life," she said. This time the wicked woman dressed herself as a peasant and, having painted her face, set out for the dwarfs' cottage with a basket of apples over her arm. There was one apple that had one rosy and one white cheek. Into the rosy cheek of this apple the queen had put deadly poison. When she reached the cottage she knocked.

"I cannot open the door to anybody," said Snowdrop from within. "The seven dwarfs have forbidden me."

"I only wanted to offer you a delicious apple," said the woman in a coaxing voice.

"I dare not take it," said Snowdrop.

"Are you afraid of being poisoned?" said the peasant, cutting the apple. "Look, I am eating one half. Won't you have the other?"

Snowdrop opened the door. The rosy cheek of the apple looked very tempting. She put out her hand and took it. She had hardly tasted it when she fell to the ground.

Then the queen laughed a harsh laugh and cried aloud, "Oh, thou who art as white as snow, as red as blood, and as black as ebony, the seven dwarfs cannot wake thee this time." And when she reached home and asked—

> Mirror, mirror on the wall,
> Am I most beautiful of all?"

the mirror replied—

> "Thou, Queen, art the fairest of beauties all."

Then at last the jealous queen was content.

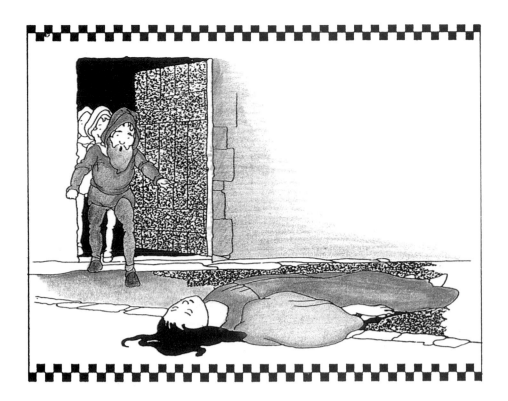

When the dwarfs came home that evening there was Snowdrop lying quite still on the floor. They cut her laces, they searched to see if there were poison about her, they combed her hair, and they washed her face with wine and water, but she never moved. Then each of the seven dwarfs said, "She is dead. Our Snowdrop is dead." And for three days and three nights the sad little men stood silently around her body. When they spoke it was only to repeat with a sigh, "She is dead. Our Snowdrop is dead."

At the end of three days the dwarfs thought they must bury her. But they could not make themselves put her beautiful rosy cheeks beneath the cold earth. So they made a coffin of glass so that they might still see her, and they wrote on the coffin in letters of gold that Snowdrop was the daughter of a king. Then the seven dwarfs carried the coffin to the top of a hill and sat by it in turn to guard it. And the wild animals and the birds and the butterflies mourned, the wild flowers drooped, and a big rain cloud wept, all because Snowdrop lay there so still.

Long months had Snowdrop lain in her glass coffin unchanged, when a king's son, having wandered through the forest, climbed the hill nearest the dwarfs' cottage. There on the top he saw the glass coffin and in it the beautiful Snowdrop.

"Let me have the coffin and I will give you for it whatever you ask," said the prince to the dwarfs.

But they answered, "Nay, we could not part with it for all the gold in the world."

"Pray, give her to me. I cannot live without seeing Snowdrop, even though she be dead," begged the prince.

At last the kind-hearted dwarfs took pity on the king's son and gave him the coffin. The prince's servants carried it down the hill, but when they reached the wood one of them stumbled over a bush. This shook Snowdrop so much that the poisoned apple fell out of her mouth and she sat up.

"Where am I?" she asked bewildered.

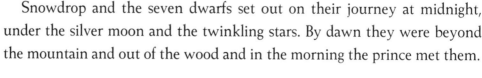

"With me," answered the prince, "and I love you so dearly that I want you to be my wife." Snowdrop said she would gladly marry the prince. Then he left her in the care of the dwarfs and asked them to bring her to his father's castle, while he rode on ahead to have everything ready.

Snowdrop and the seven dwarfs set out on their journey at midnight, under the silver moon and the twinkling stars. By dawn they were beyond the mountain and out of the wood and in the morning the prince met them.

Then Snowdrop thanked the seven dwarfs and they said good-bye to her and went home. They knew they would miss the girl, for she had brightened their lives with her merry ways. But they knew she would be safer from her cruel stepmother with the prince than with them.

The king made a grand wedding feast for the prince and Snowdrop. The wicked Queen was among those invited to it. She dressed herself in a beautiful gown and stood before the magic mirror.

> "Mirror, mirror on the wall,
> Am I most beautiful of all?"

she asked.

And the mirror answered—

> "Here, lady Queen, thou'rt the brightest star,
> But the new-crowned Queen is fairer far."

The queen was angrier than ever. At first she thought she would not go to the wedding, but she felt so curious to see who could be fairer than she that she changed her mind. When she came to the castle and found that the new-crowned queen was Snowdrop, she turned purple with rage. She became very ill, was taken home, and died soon afterward.

The prince and Snowdrop lived for many happy years. The seven dwarfs often came to see them and each time they were very sad when they had to say good-bye to their dear Snowdrop.

The Fox and the Crow

A crow was sitting on a branch of a tree with a piece of cheese in her beak when a fox observed her and set his wits to work to discover some way of getting the cheese. Coming and standing under the tree he looked up and said, "What a noble bird I see above me! Her beauty is without equal, the hue of her plumage exquisite. If only her voice is as sweet as her looks are fair, she ought without doubt to be Queen of the Birds."

The crow was hugely flattered by this, and just to show the fox that she could sing she gave a loud caw. Down came the cheese, of course, and the fox, snatching it up, said, "You have a voice, madam, I see. What you want is wits."

AESOP

The Town Mouse and the Country Mouse

A town mouse and a country mouse were acquaintances, and the country mouse one day invited his friend to come and see him at his home in the fields. The town mouse came, and they sat down to a dinner of barleycorns and roots, which had a distinctly earthy flavor. The fare was not much to the taste of the guest and presently he said, "My poor dear friend, you live here no better than the ants. Now, you should just see how I fare! My larder is a regular horn of plenty. You must come and stay with me, and I promise you you shall live on the fat of the land."

So when he returned to town he took the country mouse with him, and showed him into a larder containing flour and oatmeal and figs and honey and dates. The country mouse had never seen anything like it, and sat down to enjoy the luxuries his friend provided. But before they had well begun, the door of the larder opened and someone came in. The two mice scampered off and hid themselves in a narrow and exceedingly uncomfortable hole. Presently, when all was quiet, they ventured out again. But someone else came in, and off they scuttled again.

This was too much for the visitor. "Good-bye," said he, "I'm off. You live in the lap of luxury, I can see, but you are surrounded by dangers; whereas at home I can enjoy my simple dinner of roots and corn in peace."

AESOP

The Sleeping Beauty

NCE upon a time, in a far-off land, there lived a king and queen who longed for a baby girl. They waited and they waited and at last the queen had a little girl. She was so beautiful and the king and queen loved her so much that they decided to have a feast to show their great joy to everyone. They invited their kinsmen and nobles and friends and neighbors. But the queen said, "I will have the fairies, too, that they may be kind and good to our daughter."

Now, just as they were all sitting down to the feast, in came an old fairy who had not been invited because no one had heard anything of her for fifty years. The king, who had ordered a gold plate for each of the seven fairies that he expected, had none for the old fairy and so a china plate was set before her. This seemed to make her very angry and she muttered crossly to herself.

As the youngest of the seven good fairies listened to her muttering, she thought, This old crone will give the princess a present that will do her harm. I shall wait to give my present until after she has given hers and perhaps mine may undo the harm. Then this good fairy hid behind a curtain.

The six fairies each gave the baby girl a present.

The first said, "You shall have a beautiful face."

The second said, "You shall think beautiful thoughts."

The third said, "You shall do kind deeds."

The fourth said, "You shall dance like a fairy."

The fifth said, "You shall sing like a nightingale."

The sixth said, "You shall play the harp."

Then up got the old fairy and in a spiteful voice she said, "When you are fifteen years old you shall learn to spin and you shall prick your finger with the spindle and die."

When the guests heard this they all cried aloud and the king and queen cried loudest of all.

But out stepped the good fairy from behind the curtain and said, "Weep not, Oh King and Queen. It is true that your daughter shall spin. It is true that she shall prick her finger. It is true that she shall fall asleep. But the sleep will not be the sleep of death. In a hundred years the son of a king shall find her, wake her, and marry her." Then all the fairies vanished.

But the king hoped to save his dear child from the threatened evil so he ordered that all the spindles in the country should be bought up and burned.

In the meantime, all the gifts of the first six fairies were fulfilled. The princess was so beautiful and well-behaved and good and wise that everyone loved her.

On the day she was fifteen years old the king and queen were not at home and the princess was feeling quite bored. So she roamed about the palace by herself, until at last she came to an old tower to which there was a narrow staircase ending at a little door. In the door was a golden key and when she turned it the door sprang open. There sat an old lady busily spinning.

"What are you doing?" asked the princess.

"Spinning," said the old lady. She nodded her head, humming a tune, while buzz! went the wheel.

"How prettily that little thing turns round!" said the princess, and took the spindle and began to try to spin. But scarcely had she touched it before the wicked fairy's prophecy was fulfilled. The spindle pricked her and she fell on a couch.

She was not dead, but had only fallen into a deep sleep. And the king and the queen, who just then came home, and all their court, fell asleep, too. And the horses slept in the stables and the dogs in the courtyard fell asleep. The pigeons slept on the housetop and the flies slept upon the walls. The fire on the hearth stopped blazing and went to sleep. The spit that was turning with a goose upon it for the king's dinner stood still. And the cook who was pulling the kitchen boy by the hair, to give him a box on the ear, let him go and both fell asleep. The butler, who was slyly tasting the ale, fell asleep with the jug at his lips. And thus everything stood still and slept soundly.

A large hedge of thorns soon grew around the palace and every year it became higher and thicker, until at last the old palace was surrounded and

hidden, so that not even the roof or the chimneys could be seen. But there went a report through all the land of the beautiful sleeping Briar Rose (for so the princess was called), so that, from time to time, several kings' sons came and tried to break through into the palace. This, however, none of them could ever do.

After many years there came a king's son. An old man told him the story of the thicket of thorns and how a wonderful palace stood behind it and how a beautiful princess, called Briar Rose, lay there asleep with all her court. He told, too, how many princes had come and had tried to break through the thicket, but that none had succeeded.

The young prince said, "I will go and see this Princess Briar Rose."

Now that very day the hundred years ended. And as the prince approached the thicket he saw nothing but beautiful flowering shrubs through which he went with ease, but they shut in after him as thick as ever. He came at last to the palace. There in the courtyard lay the dogs asleep. The horses were standing in the stables. On the roof sat the pigeons fast asleep with their heads under their wings. When he came into the palace, he saw that the flies were sleeping on the walls. The spit was standing still. The butler had the jug of ale at his lips, about to drink. The maid sat with a fowl in her lap ready to be plucked. And the cook in the kitchen was still holding up her hand, as if she were going to hit the boy.

The prince continued on. All was so still that he could hear every breath he drew. At last he came to the old tower and opened the door of the little room in which Briar Rose was. And there she lay, fast asleep, on a couch near the window. She looked so beautiful that he could not take his eyes off her, so he stooped down and gave her a kiss.

The moment he kissed the princess she awoke and opened her eyes and smiled at him. And they went out together. Soon the king and queen and all the court also awoke and they gazed on each other with great wonder. And the horses shook themselves and the dogs jumped up and barked. The pigeons took their heads from under their wings, looked about, and flew into the fields. The flies on the walls buzzed again. The fire in the kitchen blazed up. And round went the spit with the goose for the king's dinner upon it. The butler finished his draught of ale. The maid went on plucking the fowl, and the cook gave the boy the box on his ear.

And then the prince and Briar Rose were married, and the wedding feast was given. And they lived happily together ever after.

Her First Pet

You ought to see my puppy eat!
    As if he'd just been starved before—
He licks the dish quite clean and neat
    Then sniffs about and whines for more.

And I am much surprised at that—
    I don't see where he puts it all.
His tummy gets so round and fat
    He's 'most as wide as he is tall.

ARTHUR ALDEN KNIPE

Picture Books In Winter.

Summer fading, winter comes—
Frosty mornings, tingling thumbs,
Window robins, winter rooks,
And the picture storybooks.

Water now is turned to stone
Nurse and I can walk upon;
Still we find the flowing brooks
In the picture storybooks.

All the pretty things put by,
Wait upon the children's eye,
Sheep and shepherds, trees and crooks,
In the picture storybooks.

We may see how all things are,
Seas and cities, near and far,
And the flying fairies' looks,
In the picture storybooks.

How am I to sing your praise,
Happy chimney-corner days,
Sitting safe in nursery nooks,
Reading picture storybooks?

ROBERT LOUIS STEVENSON

Rose-Red and Rose-White

HERE was once a poor widow who lived in a little cottage, and in front of the cottage there grew two rosebushes. One bore roses of a pure and exquisite white, the other bore red roses, rich and beautiful. And so it was that the widow's two little girls were called Rose-White and Rose-Red, because they resembled nothing so much as the flowers which blossomed in the garden. And they were good, too, and industrious and happy. Rose-White was quieter and more gentle than Rose-Red. For Rose-Red would run and jump about in the meadows, seeking flowers and catching butterflies, while Rose-White sat at home with her mother, helping her with her work or reading.

The two children loved each other dearly and always walked hand in hand when they went out together. And they agreed that they would never separate and that what one had would always be shared with the other.

Often they ran deep into the forest, to gather wild berries, but no animal ever harmed them. The rabbits came to eat lettuce out of their hands, the deer grazed by their sides, the foxes played about them, and even the birds perched on a bough beside them and sang as if no one were near. If it grew dark while they were in the forest, they lay down upon the moss and slept until morning. And because their mother knew that they would do so, she did not worry about them.

Rose-White and Rose-Red kept their mother's cottage so clean that it was a joy to enter it. Every morning, in the summertime, Rose-Red would first put the house in order and then place next to her mother's bed a bouquet which had in it a rose from each of the two rosebushes. Every winter's morning Rose-White would light the fire and put the kettle on to boil, and

although the kettle was made of copper, it shone like gold, because it was scoured so well.

In the evenings, when the snow was falling, the mother would say, "Go, Rose-White, and bolt the door. And then they would sit down on the hearth together and the mother would read to them while the little girls were spinning. By their side lay a lamb, and on a perch behind them sat a little white dove with its head tucked under its wing.

One evening, as they were all sitting happily together in this way, there came a knock at the door, as if someone wished to enter.

"Make haste, Rose-Red!" said her mother. "Open the door. Perhaps it is some traveler seeking shelter."

So Rose-Red went and drew the bolt and opened the door, expecting to see some poor man standing there. But it was nothing of the kind. It was a great black bear and he poked his big head in at the open door. Rose-Red sprang back, the little lamb bleated, the dove fluttered its wings, and Rose-White ran and hid behind her mother's chair.

"Do not be afraid," the bear said, in a rough but kind voice. "I will do you no harm. I am half-frozen, and would like to warm myself a little at your fire."

"Poor bear!" said the mother. "Come in and lie down before the fire. But take care you do not burn your fur." Then she turned to her children. "Come here, Rose-Red and Rose-White. The bear will not harm you."

So the little girls both came back and the lamb and the dove also overcame their fears and welcomed the rough visitor.

"Children," said the bear, as he stood in the doorway, "please knock some of the snow off my coat."

And they brought their little brooms and swept the bear's coat quite clean.

After that he stretched himself out in front of the fire and occasionally growled a little, only to show that he was happy and comfortable. Before long they were all quite good friends and the children began to play with their big

Florence Choate

visitor. They pulled his long shaggy fur, sat upon his back, and rolled him over and over. And he bore it all very good-naturedly.

When it was bedtime, the mother said to the bear, "You may sleep here on the hearth if you like, so that you will be sheltered from the cold and the bad weather."

The bear said that he would be glad to do so. When morning came he asked the two children to let him out and away he trotted over the snow, into the great woods.

After this, every evening at the same time the bear came, lay by the fire, and allowed the children to play with him. They soon became quite fond of their unusual playmate and the door was always left unbolted until their shaggy friend arrived.

But one morning when spring returned and everything outdoors was green again, the bear told Rose-White that he must leave them and could not return during the whole summer.

"Where are you going, then, dear bear?" asked Rose-White.

"I am obliged to go into the forest and guard my treasures from the evil dwarfs. In winter, when the ground is hard, these treasures are safe under the frozen earth, but now the warm sun will melt the ice and it will be easy for the dwarfs to dig down and reach what is mine. And what has once passed into their hands, and gets hidden by them in their caves, is not easily brought to light."

Rose-White was very sad at the departure of the good bear. She opened the door so hesitatingly that when he pressed through it he left behind on the latch a piece of his coat. Through the hole which was made in his fur Rose-White thought she saw the glittering of gold, but she was not quite certain of it.

One day, not long after this, the mother sent the girls into the woods to gather twigs. While they were doing so they came to a tree which was lying across the path. Near the trunk of the tree they saw something bobbing up and down in the grass. They could not imagine what it could be. As they came nearer, however, they saw that it was a dwarf with an old and wrinkled face and a snow-white beard that was at least a yard long. The end of this beard was held tight in a split in the tree and the little man kept jumping about like a dog tied by a chain, for he did not know how to free himself. He glared at the children with his red, fiery eyes.

"Why do you stand there?" he cried. "Can't you come and try to help me?"

"What were you doing, little fellow?" inquired Rose-Red.

"Stupid, inquisitive goose!" he exclaimed. "I meant to split the tree, so that I could chop it up for kindling. I had driven the wedge in properly, and everything was going very well, when the wedge flew upward and the tree closed so suddenly that I could not pull out my beautiful beard. And now here I must stay; for I cannot set myself free. Don't stand there and laugh, you stupid, pale-faced creatures!"

In spite of the dwarf's bad temper, the little girls did everything they could to release him; but without success.

"I will run and get some help," said Rose-Red.

"Idiot!" cried the dwarf. "Why should you call more people? Already there are two too many. Can't you think of something else?"

"Do not be impatient," said Rose-White. "I have thought of something."

And, pulling her little sewing scissors out of her pocket, she cut off the end of the beard.

As soon as the dwarf found himself free, he snatched up his sack, which lay hidden among the roots of the tree, and throwing it over his shoulder marched off, grumbling and groaning to himself, "Stupid creatures! To cut off a piece of my beautiful beard!" And away he went, without once looking back at the children.

Not long after this, Rose-Red and Rose-White went down to the brook to catch a fish for dinner. As they drew near the water, they saw something like a great grasshopper hopping about the bank as if it wished to jump into the brook. They ran up and found it was the dwarf.

"What are you doing?" cried Rose-Red. "You will fall into the water!"

"I am not such a simpleton as that!" replied the dwarf. "But don't you see that this fish will pull me in?"

The little man had been sitting on the bank fishing and, unfortunately, the wind had entangled his long white beard with the line. When a great fish took the bait, the little fellow was not strong enough to draw the fish out and now he was being dragged, little by little, into the brook.

With both hands, the dwarf held on to the reeds and rushes which grew near, but to no avail, for the fish pulled him where it liked.

The children tried to untangle his long beard, but they were unable to do so. Then Rose-White pulled out her scissors again and cut off another piece of the beard.

When the dwarf was freed and saw what had been done, he was in a great rage.

"You donkey!" he cried. "You are trying to disfigure my face! It was not enough that you cut off one piece, but now you must take away the best part of my fine beard! I dare not show myself again to my people. I wish you had got lost upon the road and not come here!"

So saying, he took up a bag, which lay among the rushes and, without speaking another word, slipped off and disappeared behind a stone.

A few days after this adventure, the widow sent the two children to the nearest town to buy thread, needles and pins, lace and ribbon. The road ran through a meadow, and in every direction great boulders were scattered about. As the children skipped along the road they saw, just over their heads, a large bird flying round and round, and every now and then dropping lower and lower until at last it flew down behind a rock. Immediately afterward they heard a piercing shriek and, running quickly to the place, they saw with horror that the great eagle had seized their old acquaintance, the dwarf, and was about to fly off with him.

The kind children did not hesitate for an instant. They grabbed hold of the dwarf and held on so tightly that at last the eagle gave up the struggle and flew away.

As soon as the dwarf had recovered from his fright, he exclaimed in his squeaking voice, "Couldn't you have held me more gently? See my fine brown coat! You have torn it, you meddling and interfering things!"

With these words, he picked up his sack and slipped away behind the rocks.

By this time Rose-Red and Rose-White were quite used to his ungrateful, ungracious ways, so they took no notice of it, but went on their way to the town, made their purchases, and started homeward again.

Now, as they passed over this same meadow, they once more came quite suddenly upon the dwarf. In a clearing he had emptied his sack, which was full of rubies and diamonds, so that he could count and admire them, for he did not imagine that anyone would be coming across the meadow at so late an hour. The setting sun was shining upon the brilliant stones and the children paused to admire their changing hues and sparkling rays.

"What are you staring at?" cried the dwarf, his face getting purple with rage. "And what are you—"

But he did not finish his abuse of them, for suddenly a great roar was heard and a moment later a big black bear came running toward them from out of the forest.

The dwarf jumped up, in terror. But before he could reach his hiding place the bear was upon him, and he cried out, in his quaking, squeaking voice, "Spare me, my dear Lord Bear! I will give you all my treasures. Just see those beautiful jewels lying there! Only grant me my life! What would you do with such a little fellow? You would not notice me between your big teeth. But see those two nice, plump children. They would make delicate morsels. Eat them, I beg of you, Mr. Bear, and let me go!"

The bear, however, without troubling himself to speak, gave the bad-hearted dwarf a blow with his huge paw and he never stirred again.

The children started to run away, making off for home as fast as they could go, but the bear called after them, "Rose-White and Rose-Red, do not be afraid. Wait a bit and I will go with you."

They recognized his voice and realized that it was their old friend.

The bear quickly came toward them, but as he reached them the bearskin suddenly dropped to the ground and there stood a handsome young man, dressed entirely in gold.

"I am a king's son," he said, "and I was enchanted by that wicked dwarf. He stole all my treasures and condemned me to wander about the forest in the form of a bear until his death should set me free. Now he has received well-deserved punishment."

They went home together and some time afterward Rose-White was married to the prince and Rose-Red was married to his brother and they shared the immense treasure which the dwarf had collected in his cave.

The mother spent many happy years with her children. The two rosebushes which had stood before the cottage were planted now before the palace and continued to bear, each year, the most beautiful red and white roses.

Beauty and the Beast

HERE was once a merchant who had six children, three boys and three girls. The three daughters were all handsome, but the youngest was so beautiful that everyone had always called her Beauty, which made her sisters extremely jealous. Not only was this youngest daughter more beautiful than her sisters, but she was better-tempered, too.

As the result of a misfortune, the merchant suddenly lost his fortune and had nothing left but a small cottage in the country. He said to his sons and daughters, the tears running down his cheeks, "My children, we must go and live in the cottage and try to work the land, for we have no other means of support left!"

After they had moved to their cottage, the merchant and his three sons worked in the fields and garden, so that they would have food for their table. Beauty rose early every morning, lit the fire, cleaned the house, and prepared the breakfast for the whole family. When she had finished her work she amused herself with reading, playing on the harpsichord, or singing as she spun. Her sisters however, breakfasted in bed and did not rise until ten. They would go for a walk, but, finding themselves very soon tired, they would frequently sit down under a shade tree and lament the loss of their carriage and fine clothes.

The family lived in this manner for about a year when the merchant received a letter, which informed him that one of his richest vessels, which he thought lost, had arrived in port. The two elder sisters were overjoyed.

When their father explained that he must take a journey to the ship they begged him to bring them on his return some new gowns, caps, rings, and all kinds of trinkets. Beauty asked for nothing; for she thought that the ship's cargo would scarcely purchase all that her sisters wished for.

"You, Beauty," said the merchant, "ask for nothing. What can I bring you?"

"Since you are so kind as to think of me, dear Father," she answered, "I should be pleased if you would bring me a rose, for we have none in our garden."

The merchant set out on his journey. When he arrived at the port, some dishonest people claimed to own the cargo. So after a great deal of trouble he returned to his cottage as poor as he had left it.

When he was within a few miles of his home and thinking of the happiness he should enjoy in again embracing his children, his road lay through a thick forest and he became lost. All at once, down a long avenue, he saw a light, but it seemed at a great distance. He rode toward it and soon saw a splendid palace brilliantly illuminated. When he reached the palace, he was surprised to find not a single creature in any of the outer yards. His horse, which followed him, finding a stable with the door open, entered, and, being nearly starved, helped himself to a plentiful meal of oats and hay. The merchant than tied him up and walked toward the house, which he entered, without, to his great astonishment, seeing a living creature. He entered a large hall in which there was a roaring fire and a table, with the most delicate dishes, on which a single place was set.

Since snow and rain had wet him to the skin, he approached the fire. "I hope," he said to himself, "that the master of the house will excuse the liberty I take, for it surely will not be long before someone makes an appearance."

He waited a considerable time and still nobody came. Finally, the clock struck eleven and the merchant, overcome with hunger and thirst, helped himself to some food, and to a few glasses of wine, all the time trembling with fear. He sat until the clock struck twelve and not a creature had he seen. He now took courage and decided to look a little farther about him. Accordingly, he opened a door at the end of the hall and entered an apartment, magnificently furnished, which opened into another in which there was an excellent bed. Quite overcome with fatigue, he decided to shut the door, undress, and get into bed. It was ten o'clock the next morning before he awoke. How astonished he was to see a handsome suit of clothes entirely new, in place of his own, which had been ruined!

"No doubt," he said to himself, "this palace belongs to some good fairy who has taken pity on my unfortunate situation."

He looked out the window and, instead of snow, he saw the most delightful flowers. He returned to the hall where he had eaten and found a breakfast table, laden with food, with one place set.

"Truly, my good fairy," said the merchant aloud, "I am extremely indebted to you for your kind care of me."

After eating a hearty breakfast, he took his hat and walked toward the stable to saddle his horse for the trip home. As he passed under one of the arbors, which was covered with beautiful roses, he remembered Beauty's request and picked a flower to take to her. At that instant he heard a most horrible noise and saw a hideous beast approaching him.

"Ungrateful man!" said the beast in a terrible voice. "I have saved your life by welcoming you to my palace and in return you steal one of my roses, which I value more than all my other possessions. With your life you shall pay for this."

The merchant fell on his knees and said, "My lord, I humbly beg your pardon. I did not think it could offend you to pick a rose for one of my daughters."

"I am not a lord, but a beast," replied the monster. "I do not like compliments, so do not imagine you can move me with your flattery. You say, however, that you have daughters. I will pardon you, on condition that one of them shall come here and live with me. Do not attempt to argue with

me, but go. If your daughters should refuse, swear to me that you will return in three months."

The merchant had no intention of letting one of his daughters return, but he thought that by seeming to accept the beast's condition, he would have the pleasure of seeing them once again. He accordingly swore, and the beast told him he might leave as soon as he pleased. "But," added he, "you should not go empty-handed. Go back to the chamber in which you slept. There you will find an empty chest. Fill it with whatever you like best and I will have it conveyed to your own house."

The beast then went away and the good merchant said to himself, "If I must die, I shall at least have the consolation of leaving my children some provision."

He returned to the chamber in which he had slept; and finding a great quantity of pieces of gold, filled the chest with them to the very brim, locked it and, mounting his horse, left the palace. The horse took a path across the forest and in a few hours they reached the merchant's house. His children gathered around him as he dismounted, but the merchant, instead of embracing them with joy, could not, as he looked at them, refrain from weeping. He held in his hand the rose, which he gave to Beauty, saying, "Take this rose, Beauty. Little do you know how much it has cost your unhappy father." He then gave an account of all that had happened in the palace of the beast.

The two eldest sisters immediately began to shed tears and to reproach Beauty, who they said would be the cause of her father's death. "See," they said, "the consequence of the pride of the little wretch. Why did she not ask for fine things as we did? But she must distinguish herself. And though she will be the cause of her father's death she does not shed a tear."

"It would be useless," replied Beauty, "to weep for the death of my father because he will not die. Since the beast will accept one of his daughters, I will go. And most happy do I think myself in being able at once to save his life and prove my love for the best of fathers."

"No, sister," said one of the three brothers, "you shall not go. We will go in search of this monster and he or we will perish."

"Do not hope to kill him," said the merchant. "His power is by far too great for this to be possible. I am touched by Beauty's kindness, but I will not permit her to risk her life. I am old and cannot expect to live much longer. I shall, therefore, have lost but a few years of my life, which I regret only for my children's sake."

"Never, my father," cried Beauty, "shall you go to the palace without me. You cannot prevent my following you."

The merchant tried in vain to reason with Beauty, for she was determined to go. He was, indeed, so distressed at the idea of losing his child that he did not think of the chest filled with gold. But going to his chamber at night, to his great surprise, he saw it standing by his bedside. He now determined to say nothing to his eldest daughters of the riches he possessed; for he knew very well they would immediately wish to return to town. But he told Beauty his secret. She told him that two gentlemen who had a great affection for her two sisters, had been visiting at their cottage during his absence. She begged her father to marry them without delay, for she was so sweet-tempered that she loved them despite their unkind behavior.

When the three months had passed, the merchant and Beauty prepared to set out for the palace of the beast. The sisters and the brothers wept, but Beauty did not cry and tried to assure them that she would be all right.

Beauty and her father reached the palace in a few hours. The horse, without bidding, entered the stable and the merchant with his daughter proceeded to the large hall where they found a table provided with every delicacy and with two places laid on it. The merchant had little appetite, but Beauty sat down at the table and, having served her father, began to eat. When they had finished their supper they heard a great noise. The good old man began to bid his poor child farewell, for he knew it was the beast coming to them. Beauty, on seeing the beast, could not help trembling, but she tried as much as possible to conceal her fear. The monster asked her if she had come willingly. She replied, trembling still more, "Y-e-s."

"You are a good girl," he replied, "and I think myself much obliged to you. Good man," he continued, "you may leave the palace tomorrow morning, and take care to return to it no more. Good night, Beauty!"

"Good night, Beast!" she answered and the monster left.

"Ah! dear child," said the merchant, embracing her, "I am distressed at the thought of leaving you here. Believe me, you had better go back and let me stay."

"No," replied Beauty firmly, "to this I will never consent. You must go home tomorrow morning."

They wished each other a sorrowful good night and went to bed, thinking it would be impossible for them to close their eyes. But no sooner had they lain down, than they each fell into a deep sleep from which they did not awake until morning. Beauty dreamed that a lady approached her, who said, "I am much pleased, Beauty, with the generous affection you have shown in being willing to give your life to save that of your father. It shall not go unrewarded."

Beauty related this dream to her father, but, though it gave him some comfort, he could not take leave of his darling child without shedding bitter tears. When the merchant was out of sight, Beauty sat down in the large hall and began to cry, too. But since she had a great deal of courage she soon resolved not to make her unhappy condition still worse by useless sorrow. She decided to explore different parts of the palace. What was her surprise at coming to a door on which was written "Beauty's apartment"! She opened it hastily, and her eyes were dazzled by the splendor of everything it contained. But the things that more than all the rest excited her wonder were a large library of books, a harpsichord, and music.

"The beast is determined I shall not want for amusement," she said to herself. She began to think that the beast was very kind and that she had nothing to fear. About noon she found a table prepared, and a delightful

concert of music played while she ate her lunch without her seeing a single creature. At supper, when she was going to seat herself at the table, she heard the noise of the beast and could not help trembling with terror.

"Will you allow me, Beauty," said he, "the pleasure of watching you sup?"

"That is as you please," she answered.

"Not in the least," said the beast, "and the beast you alone command. If you dislike my company, you have only to say so and I shall leave you. But tell me, Beauty, do you not think me very ugly?"

"Truly, yes," replied she, "for I cannot tell a falsehood; but I think you are very good."

"You are right," continued the beast. "And, besides my ugliness, I am also ignorant. I know well enough that I am but a beast. But pray do not let me interrupt you eating," he said, "and be sure you do not want for anything, for all you see is yours and I shall be grieved if you are not happy."

"You are very good," replied Beauty. "I must confess I think very highly of your disposition; and that makes me almost forget your ugliness."

"Yes, I trust I am good-tempered," he said, "but still I am a monster."

"Many men are more monsters than you," replied Beauty. "And I am better pleased with you in that form, ugly as it is, than with those who, under the form of men, conceal wicked hearts."

"If I had any understanding," resumed the beast, "I would thank you for what you have said, but I am too stupid to say anything that could give you pleasure."

Beauty ate with an excellent appetite and had nearly conquered her fear of the monster. But she was ready to sink with horror when he said, "Beauty, will you be my wife?"

She was afraid of making him angry by refusing and remained silent for a few moments before saying, "No, Beast."

The beast sighed deeply and said, in a melancholy tone, "Adieu, Beauty!" and left her, turning his head two or three times as he went to look at her. Beauty, finding herself alone, began to feel the greatest compassion for the poor beast.

"Alas!" she said to herself, "what a pity it is he should be so very frightful, since he is so good-tempered!"

Beauty lived three months in the palace, very contentedly. The beast visited her every evening and entertained her with his conversation while she ate. Though what he said was not very clever, every day Beauty saw new virtues in him and, instead of dreading the time of his coming, she continually looked at her watch to see if it was almost nine o'clock, at which time he never failed to visit her. There was only one thing that made her uneasy. The beast, before he retired, constantly asked her if she would be his wife and appeared extremely sorrowful at her refusals.

One day, Beauty said to him, "You distress me exceedingly, Beast, in obliging me to refuse you so often. I wish I could prevail on myself to marry you, but I am too sincere to flatter you that this will ever happen."

"I love you exceedingly," replied the beast. "However, I think myself fortunate in your being pleased to stay with me. Promise me, Beauty, that you will never leave me."

"I would willingly promise," said she, "never to leave you entirely. But I have such a longing desire to see my father that if you refuse me this pleasure I shall die of grief."

"Rather would I die myself, Beauty," he replied, "than cause you sadness. I will send you to your father's cottage. You shall stay there and your poor beast shall die of grief."

"No," said Beauty, weeping, "I love you too well to be the cause of your death. I promise to return in a week. I know that by now my sisters are married and my brothers have gone to the army. My father is, therefore, all alone. Allow me to spend one week with him."

"You shall find yourself with him tomorrow morning," answered the beast. "But remember your promise. When you wish to return you have only to put your ring on a table when you go to bed. Adieu, Beauty!"

The beast sighed and when Beauty went to bed she was extremely sad that he was so distressed. When she awoke in the morning, she found herself in her father's cottage. Ringing a bell that was at her bedside, a servant entered and, on seeing her, gave a loud shriek.

The merchant ran upstairs and, on beholding his daughter, was ready to die of joy. They embraced again and again.

Finally, Beauty realized that she had no clothes to put on, but the servant told her she had just found a large chest filled with apparel, embroidered with gold and ornamented with pearls and diamonds. Beauty thanked the kind beast in her thoughts for his attention, and dressed herself in the plainest of

the gowns, telling the servant to put away the others carefully for she intended to present them to her sisters. But scarcely had she pronounced these words than the chest disappeared. Her father observed that no doubt the beast intended she should keep everything for herself. Immediately the chest returned to the same place.

While Beauty was dressing, notice was sent to her sisters of her arrival. They lost no time in coming with their husbands to pay her a visit. The two sisters were ready to burst with envy when they saw Beauty dressed like a princess and looking so very beautiful. All the kindness she showed them produced not the least effect. Their jealousy was increased when she told them how happily she lived at the palace of the beast. The envious creatures went secretly into the garden, where they cried with spite to think of her good fortune.

"Sister," said the eldest, "let us try to keep her here beyond the week allowed by the beast; who will then be so enraged, that ten to one but he eats her up in a moment."

Having decided on this, they joined her in the cottage and showed her so much affection that Beauty could not help crying for joy. When the week was ended, the two sisters began to tear their hair and pretend so much sadness at the thought of her leaving them that she consented to stay another week. But during that week Beauty could not help constantly reproaching herself for the unhappiness she knew she must be causing her poor beast, whom she tenderly loved and for whose company she much wished. On the tenth night she was at the cottage, she dreamed she was in the garden of the palace and that the beast lay expiring, and in a dying voice reproached her with ingratitude. Beauty awoke and burst into tears.

"Am I not very wicked," she said, "to act so unkindly to a beast who has treated me with such kindness? It is not his fault that he is ugly and stupid. And he is so good! Which is far better than all the rest. Why do I refuse to marry him? I should certainly be happier with him than my sisters with their husbands, for it is kindness, virtue, and obliging temper which makes a wife happy and all these qualities the beast certainly has. I do not love him, but I feel the sincerest friendship, esteem, and gratitude for him."

She put her ring on the table and soon fell asleep again. In the morning she found herself in the beast's palace. She put on her prettiest gown that she might please him the better and thought she had never passed so long a day. Finally the clock struck nine, but no beast appeared. Beauty imagined she had been the cause of his death. She ran from room to room all over the palace, calling his name in despair. But still no beast came. After searching for a long time, she remembered her dream and instantly ran toward the grass plot on which she had seen him. And there she found the poor beast lying senseless and to all appearance dead. She threw herself upon his body, thinking nothing at all of his ugliness. Finding that his heart still beat, she ran hastily and fetched some water and threw it on his face.

The beast opened his eyes, and said, "You forgot your promise, Beauty. My grief for the loss of you made me resolve to starve myself to death. At least I shall die content, since I have had the pleasure of seeing you once more."

"No, dear Beast," replied Beauty, "you shall not die. You shall live to become my husband. From this moment I offer you my hand, and swear to be only yours. Alas! I thought I felt only friendship for you, but the pain I feel convinces me that I could not live without seeing you."

Scarcely had Beauty pronounced these words before the palace was suddenly illuminated and music, fireworks, and all kinds of amusements announced the most splendid rejoicings. This, however, had no effect on Beauty, who watched over her dear beast with the most tender anxiety. But what was her amazement to see all at once at her feet a handsome prince who thanked her with the utmost tenderness for having broken his enchantment! She could not refrain from asking him what had become of the beast.

"You see him, Beauty, at your feet," answered the prince. "A wicked fairy had condemned me to keep the form of a beast until a beautiful young lady should consent to marry me, and had forbidden me on pain of death to show that I had any understanding. You alone, dearest Beauty, have had the generosity to judge me by the goodness of my heart."

Beauty, in the most pleasing surprise, helped the handsome prince to rise and they proceeded together to the palace. Her astonishment was very great to find waiting there her father and all her family, who had been conveyed to the palace by the beautiful lady she saw in her dream.

"Beauty," said the lady (for she was a great fairy), "receive the reward of the virtuous choice you have made. You have preferred goodness of heart to sense and beauty: you therefore deserve to find these qualities united in the same person. You are going to be a great queen."

Beauty and the prince were married and lived happily ever after.

MY KINGDOM

Down by a shining water well
I found a very little dell,
    No higher than my head.
The heather and the gorse about
In summer bloom were coming out,
    Some yellow and some red.

I called the little pool a sea;
The little hills were big to me,
    For I am very small.
I made a boat, I made a town,
I searched the caverns up and down,
    And named them one and all.

And all about was mine, I said,
The little sparrows overhead,
   The little minnows too.
This was the world and I was king;
For me the bees came by to sing,
   For me the swallows flew.

I played there were no deeper seas,
Nor any wider plains than these,
   Nor other kings than me.
At last I heard my mother call
Out from the house at evenfall,
   To call me home to tea.

And I must rise and leave my dell,
And leave my dimpled water well,
   And leave my heather blooms.
Alas! and as my home I neared,
How very big my nurse appeared,
   How great and cool the rooms!
                    ROBERT LOUIS STEVENSON

The Bear Story

That Alex "ist maked up his-own-se'f"

W'y, wunst they wuz a Little Boy went out
In the woods to shoot a Bear. So, he went out
'Way in the grea'-big woods—he did.—An' he
Wuz goin' along—an' goin' along, you know,
An' purty soon he heerd somepin' go *"Wooh!"*—
Ist thataway—*"Woo-ooh!"* An' he wuz *skeered*,
He wuz. An' so he runned an' clumbed a tree—
A grea'-big tree, he did,—a sicka-*more* tree.
An' nen he heerd it ag'in: an' he looked round,
An' *'t'uz a Bear!—a grea'-big shore-'nuff Bear!*—
No: 't'uz *two* Bears, it wuz—two grea'-big Bears—
One of 'em wuz—ist *one's* a *grea'-big* Bear.—
But they ist *boff* went *"Wooh!"*—An' here *they* come
To climb the tree an' git the Little Boy
An' eat him up!

An' nen the Little Boy
He 'uz skeered worse'n ever! An' here come
The grea'-big Bear a-climbin' th' tree to git
The Little Boy an' eat him up—Oh, *no!*—
It 'uzn't the *Big* Bear 'at clumb the tree—
It 'uz the *Little* Bear. So here *he* come
Climbin' the tree—an' climbin' the tree! Nen when
He git wite *clos't* to the Little Boy, w'y, nen
The Little Boy he ist pulled up his gun
An' *shot* the Bear, he did, an' killed him dead!
An' nen the Bear he falled clean on down out
The tree—away clean to the ground, he did—
Spling-splung! he falled *plum* down, an' killed him, too!
An' lit wite side o' where the *Big* Bear's at.

An' nen the Big Bear's awful mad, you bet!—
'Cause—'cause the Little Boy he shot his gun
An' killed the *Little* Bear.—'Cause the *Big* Bear
He—he 'uz the Little Bear's Papa.—An' so here
He come to climb the big old tree an' git
The Little Boy an' eat him up! An' when
The Little Boy he saw the *grea'-big Bear*
A-comin', he uz badder skeered, he wuz,
Than *any* time! An' so he think he'll climb
Up *higher*—'way up higher in the tree
Than the old *Bear* kin climb, you know.—But he—
He *can't* climb higher 'an old *Bears* kin climb,—
'Cause Bears kin climb up higher in the trees
Than any little Boys in all the Wo-r-r-ld!

An' so here come the grea'-big Bear, he did,—
A-climbin' up—an' up the tree, to git
The Little Boy an' eat him up! An' so
The Little Boy he clumbed on higher, an' higher,
An' higher up the tree—an' higher—an' higher—
An' higher'n iss-here *house* is!—An' here come
The old Bear—clos'ter to him all the time!—
An' nen—first thing you know,—when th' old Big Bear
Wuz wite clos't to him—nen the Little Boy
Ist jabbed his gun wite in the old Bear's mouf
An' shot an' killed him dead!—No; I *fergot,*—
He didn't shoot the grea'-big Bear at all—
'Cause *they 'uz no load in the gun,* you know—
'Cause when he shot the *Little* Bear, w'y, nen
No load 'uz any more nen *in* the gun!

But th' Little Boy clumbed *higher* up, he did—
He clumbed *lots* higher—an' on up *higher*—an' higher
An' *higher*—tel he ist *can't* climb no higher,
'Cause nen the limbs 'uz all so little, 'way
Up in the teeny-weeny tip-top of
The tree, they'd break down wiv him ef he don't
Be keerful! So he stop an' think: An' nen
He look around—An' here come the old Bear!
An' so the Little Boy make up his mind
He's got to ist git out o' there *someway!*—
'Cause here come the old Bear!—so clos't, his bref's
Purt' nigh so's he kin feel how hot it is
Ag'inst his bare feet—ist like old "Ring's" bref
When he's be'n out a-huntin' an' 's all tired.

So when th' old Bear's so clos't—the Little Boy
Ist gives a grea'-big jump fer 'nother tree—
No!—no, he don't do that!—I tell you what
The Little Boy does:—W'y, nen—w'y, he—Oh, *yes!*—
The Little Boy *he finds a hole up there*
'At's in the tree—an' climbs in there an' *hides*—
An' *nen* th' old Bear can't find the Little Boy
At all!—but purty soon the old Bear finds
The Little Boy's *gun* 'at's up there—'cause the *gun*
It's too *tall* to tooked wiv him in the hole.
So, when the old Bear find' the *gun*, he knows
The Little Boy's ist *hid* round *somers* there,—
An' th' old Bear 'gins to snuff an' sniff around,
An' sniff an' snuff around—so's he kin find
Out where the Little Boy's hid at.—An' nen—nen—
Oh, *yes!*—W'y, purty soon the old Bear climbs
'Way out on a big limb—a grea'-long limb,—
An' nen the Little Boy climbs out the hole
An' takes his ax an' chops the limb off! . . . Nen
The old Bear falls *k-splunge!* clean to the ground,
An' bu'st an' kill hisse'f plum dead, he did!

An' nen the Little Boy he git his gun
An' 'menced a-climbin' down the tree ag'in—
No!—no, he *didn't* git his *gun*—'cause when
The *Bear* falled, nen the *gun* falled, too—An' broked
It all to pieces, too!—An' *nicest* gun!—
His Pa ist buyed it!—An' the Little Boy
Ist cried, he did; an' went on climbin' down
The tree—an' climbin' down—an' climbin' down!—

An'-sir! when he 'uz purt' nigh down,—w'y, nen
The old Bear he jumped up ag'in!—an' he
Ain't dead at all—*ist* 'tendin' thataway,
So he kin git the Little Boy an' eat
Him up! But the Little Boy he 'uz too smart
To climb clean *down* the tree.—An' the old Bear
He can't climb *up* the tree no more—'cause when
He fell, he broke one of his—He broke *all*
His legs!—an' nen he *couldn't* climb! But he
Ist won't go 'way an' let the Little Boy
Come down out of the tree. An' the old Bear
Ist growls round there, he does—ist growls an' goes
"*Wooh!—woo-ooh!*" all the time! An' Little Boy
He haf to stay up in the tree—all night—
An' 'thout no *supper* neever!—Only they
Wuz *apples* on the tree!—An' Little Boy
Et apples—ist all night—an' cried—an' cried!
Nen when 't'uz morning the old Bear went "*Wooh!*"
Ag'in, an' try to climb up in the tree
An' git the Little Boy—But he *can't*
Climb t' save his *soul*, he can't!—An' oh! he's *mad!*—
He ist tear up the ground! an' go "*Woo-ooh!*"
An'—*Oh, yes!*—purty soon, when morning's come
All *light*—so's you kin *see*, you know,—w'y, nen
The old Bear finds the Little Boy's *gun*, you know,
'At's on the ground.—(An' it ain't broke at all—
I ist *said* that!) An' so the old Bear think
He'll take the gun an' *shoot* the Little Boy:—
But *Bears they* don't know much 'bout shootin' guns:

So when he go to shoot the Little Boy,
The old Bear got the *other* end the gun
Ag'in' his shoulder, 'stid o' *th' other* end—
So when he try to shoot the Little Boy,
It shot *the Bear,* it did—an' killed him dead!
An' nen the Little Boy clumb down the tree
An' chopped his old woolly head off.—Yes, an' killed
The *other* Bear ag'in, he did—an' killed
All *boff* the bears, he did—an' tuk 'em home
An' *cooked* 'em, too, an' *et* 'em!

                              —An' that's all.
                    JAMES WHITCOMB RILEY

Daffodils

I wandered lonely as a cloud
 That floats on high o'er vales and hills,
When all at once I saw a crowd,
 A host of golden daffodils
Beside the lake, beneath the trees,
Fluttering and dancing in the breeze.

Continuous as the stars that shine
 And twinkle on the Milky Way,
They stretched in never-ending line
 Along the margin of a bay:
Ten thousand saw I, at a glance,
Tossing their heads in sprightly dance.

The waves beside them danced, but they
 Outdid the sparkling waves in glee;
A poet could not be but gay
 In such a jocund company;
I gazed—and gazed—but little thought
What wealth the show to me had brought.

For oft, when on my couch I lie,
 In vacant or in pensive mood,
They flash upon that inward eye
 Which is the bliss of solitude;
And then my heart with pleasure fills,
And dances with the daffodils.

WILLIAM WORDSWORTH

BED IN SUMMER

In winter I get up at night
And dress by yellow candlelight.
In summer, quite the other way,
I have to go to bed by day.

I have to go to bed and see
The birds still hopping on the tree,
Or hear the grown-up people's feet
Still going past me in the street.

And does it not seem hard to you,
When all the sky is clear and blue,
And I should like so much to play,
To have to go to bed by day?

ROBERT LOUIS STEVENSON

My Garden

I keep my garden neat and trim
　　And pluck out every weed;
Though now and then the summer sun
　　Is very hot indeed.

I rake and smooth the soil with care,
　　Which takes a lot of pains,
And water every plant each day—
　　Excepting when it rains.

For all the flowers seem so glad
　　When raked and watered well,
They lift their heads as if to say
　　"You'll like the way we smell."

ARTHUR ALDEN KNIPE